PRESIDENT TAFT IS STUCK IN THE BATH

Mac Barnett   *illustrated by* **Chris Van Dusen**

CANDLEWICK PRESS

But today President Taft is stuck in his bathtub.

"Blast!" said Taft. "This could be bad."

W.H.TAFT

WILLIAM HOWARD TAFT *was the twenty-seventh president of the United States. He busted monopolies, instituted the federal income tax, and became the only president to also serve as chief justice of the Supreme Court.*

He squeezed and he shimmied.

He hefted and stretched.

He gripped the rim of the tub and attempted to lift himself. But it was no use: President Taft was stuck in the bath.

Taft took a deep breath and tugged his mustache.

"Think, Taft!" said Taft. "Use that big noggin and cook up a plan!"

Two hours passed.
The water got cold.
And President Taft was still stuck in the bath.

"I hope," said Taft, "that nobody notices I am missing."

Someone knocked at the door.

"Double blast!" said Taft. "Blast and drat!"

"Willy?"

Oh, dear. It was Taft's wife, the first lady of the United States of America.

"You've been in there a while. Is everything fine?"

Taft splashed in the bath.

"Yes, Nellie!" he said. "I'm just scrubbing my back!"

"I see," Nellie said. "Are you really quite sure?"

"Oh, blast!" shouted Taft. "Why can't a man have a nice quiet bath?"

Nellie said, "Sorry, Willy."

She sniffed. Taft felt bad.

"My love," said Taft, "I am stuck in the bath."

"So you are," said Nellie. She thought. "Well, perhaps—"

"It's a disaster!" said Taft.

"Yes, but perhaps—"

"Blast 'perhaps'!" shouted Taft. "We need action. A plan! Please be a sweetie and call the vice president."

The vice president came and stood by the tub.

"Well, Jim," said Taft, "I'm stuck in the bath."

"I see," said the V.P. "Well, you've called the right man. I'm ready to be sworn in as the president of the United States of America."

"Blast that!" bellowed Taft. "A preposterous plan."

"Perhaps—" said the first lady.

"Call the secretary of state!" shouted President Taft.

"Mr. Secretary," said Taft, "I'm stuck in the bath."

"Indeed," said the secretary of state. "Let me put this diplomatically. A man of great stature need not be of great girth, and so—"

"Blast, man!" shouted Taft. "Are you calling me fat?"

"No, sir!" The secretary of state was taken aback. "But certainly a diet, combined with calisthenics—"

"Blast diets!" said Taft. "I need something fast!"

"Should we swear me in as president now?" asked the vice president.

"Call the secretary of agriculture!" shouted President Taft.

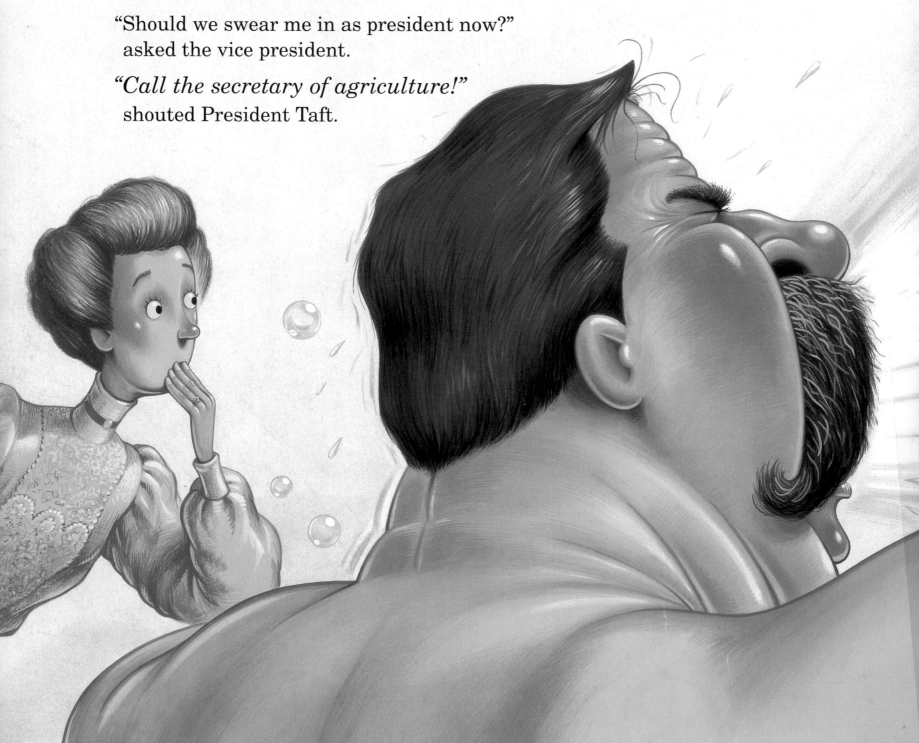

"Mr. Secretary," said Taft, "I'm stuck in the bath."

"Hmm," said the secretary. "A huge vat of butter should do the trick. We'll have fifty farmers milk fifty cows. If Congress spends the night churning, we should have enough. We'll grease up your sides and the sides of the tub. Then it will be easy. You'll slide right out!"

"Blast butter!" said Taft. "As soon as I'm out, I'll just need a bath."

"Perhaps—" said the first lady.

"*Call the secretary of war!*" shouted President Taft.

"Mr. Secretary," said Taft, "I'm stuck in the bath."

"Yes," said the secretary. "We'll soon see to that."

"With what?" Taft asked.

"Dynamite!"

Taft was aghast.

"We just need a few sticks of TNT and a rather long fuse, and —*BOOM*— you'll be free! We'll blast this old tub into smithereens!"

"Blast blasting!" said Taft. "That's dangerous, man!"

"You'd be wearing a helmet," said the secretary of war.

"No!" shouted Taft.

"Don't you think *President James Schoolcraft Sherman* sounds catchy?" said the vice president.

"No!" shouted Taft.

"Perhaps—" said the first lady.

"Call the secretaries of the navy, treasury, and interior!" shouted President Taft.

"Send deep-sea divers into the tub!"
said the secretary of the navy.

"Throw money at the problem!"
said the secretary of the treasury.

"The answer is inside you,"
said the secretary of the interior.

"Blast that, that, and that!" shouted President Taft. "It is clear: I am unfit for office. A president cannot govern while stuck in a bath. Am I to be carried around this great nation in a tub, borne aloft on the backs of six young men like a princeling from antiquity?

"NO," bellowed Taft. "IT IS UN-AMERICAN."

Taft waved his right hand. "Fetch the chief justice. I will resign. Let's swear Sherman in."

"Wait!" said the first lady.

"Let's not be rash. There are eight of us here. Perhaps if we stopped using our brains and just used our arms, we could pull Willy out from the bath."

It was a pretty good plan. And so those eight great minds rolled up their sleeves, and they yanked and they tugged. At first Taft wouldn't budge. But then came a squeak, and a slap, and a snap, and just like that . . .

President Taft flew from the bath.

There were many glad cries. Taft kissed his wife. A celebration ensued, and someone called in a band. There was dancing and snacks. The secretary of state raised his glass.

"A toast," he said, "to President Taft. Worry not, great man: One hundred years hence, no one will recall that you were stuck in the bath. Our grandchildren's grandchildren will read of your many great feats."

The crowd broke into applause.

"Speech! Speech!" they all said.

The band stopped. Taft cleared his throat. Those gathered were rapt.

"Would somebody hand me a robe?" he asked.

And that's that.

AUTHOR'S NOTE

Taft's White House tub, custom-built for the president by the J. L. Mott Iron Works of Trenton, New Jersey. Four men sit in the tub, and there looks to be room for at least two more.

Some people say President Taft got stuck in his bath on March 4, 1909, his inauguration day. Others say it happened later in his term. Depending on who's talking, it took two men to pry out the president, or four men, or four men plus a gallon of loblolly, which is butter mixed with lobster liver.

Of course, many say Taft never got stuck at all.

What follows is what we know for certain.

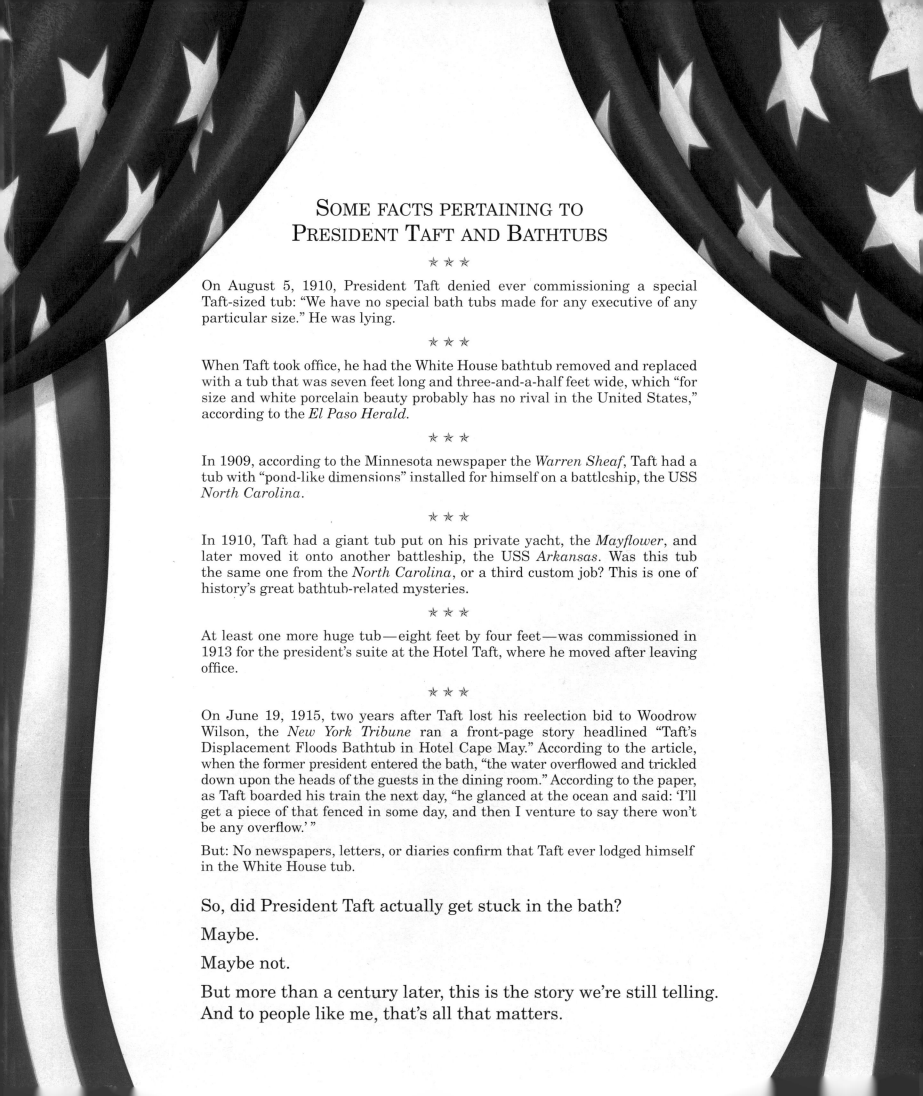

Some facts pertaining to President Taft and Bathtubs

✳ ✳ ✳

On August 5, 1910, President Taft denied ever commissioning a special Taft-sized tub: "We have no special bath tubs made for any executive of any particular size." He was lying.

✳ ✳ ✳

When Taft took office, he had the White House bathtub removed and replaced with a tub that was seven feet long and three-and-a-half feet wide, which "for size and white porcelain beauty probably has no rival in the United States," according to the *El Paso Herald*.

✳ ✳ ✳

In 1909, according to the Minnesota newspaper the *Warren Sheaf*, Taft had a tub with "pond-like dimensions" installed for himself on a battleship, the USS *North Carolina*.

✳ ✳ ✳

In 1910, Taft had a giant tub put on his private yacht, the *Mayflower*, and later moved it onto another battleship, the USS *Arkansas*. Was this tub the same one from the *North Carolina*, or a third custom job? This is one of history's great bathtub-related mysteries.

✳ ✳ ✳

At least one more huge tub—eight feet by four feet—was commissioned in 1913 for the president's suite at the Hotel Taft, where he moved after leaving office.

✳ ✳ ✳

On June 19, 1915, two years after Taft lost his reelection bid to Woodrow Wilson, the *New York Tribune* ran a front-page story headlined "Taft's Displacement Floods Bathtub in Hotel Cape May." According to the article, when the former president entered the bath, "the water overflowed and trickled down upon the heads of the guests in the dining room." According to the paper, as Taft boarded his train the next day, "he glanced at the ocean and said: 'I'll get a piece of that fenced in some day, and then I venture to say there won't be any overflow.'"

But: No newspapers, letters, or diaries confirm that Taft ever lodged himself in the White House tub.

So, did President Taft actually get stuck in the bath?

Maybe.

Maybe not.

But more than a century later, this is the story we're still telling. And to people like me, that's all that matters.

For Yaakov, Taft scholar
M. B.

For Steven Malk and his nephews
C. V.

The photograph accompanying the author's note originally appeared in the journal
Engineering Review, *February 1909. Giant thanks to J. Robert Lennon for his help. — M. B.*

First edition 2014

Library of Congress Catalog Card Number 2013943103
ISBN 978-0-7636-6317-9

13 14 15 16 17 18 TTP 10 9 8 7 6 5 4 3 2 1

Printed in Huizhou, Guangdong, China

This book was typeset in New Century Schoolbook.
The illustrations were done in gouache.

Candlewick Press
99 Dover Street
Somerville, Massachusetts 02144

visit us at www.candlewick.com